How You Got So SMART

by David Milgrim

SCHOLASTIC INC.
New York Toronto London Auckland
Sydney Mexico City New Delhi Hong Kong

Just look at you now.
You've come very far.
You're as sharp as a tack,
You're as bright as a star,

You've made us all proud
by who you've become,
and we'd like to review
how you did what you've done.

You watched the world closely.

You studied the sounds.

You had a small taste

of whatever you found.

You wandered and wondered.
You loved to explore.

For every answer you got,
you had three questions more.

You loved a good mystery.

You prodded and poked.

You knew how to listen
when anyone spoke.

You made a few friends.
You learned how to share.

You were never afraid
to show that you care.

You gave things a try.
You were brave and courageous.

You liked to do things
that were wild and outrageous.

You loved to be challenged.
You wanted to fly.

The more that you failed,
the harder you tried.

You put things together
to see what they made.

When life gave you lemons,
you made lemonade.

You learned it's okay
if you cry when you're sad

and how to express yourself
when you are mad.

You had many teachers.
You learned from them well.

You had your own stories
you needed to tell.

You played your own music.
You sang with your heart.

And look at you now . . .
you're so brilliantly smart.

You got where you're going.
You did it your way.

For all the geniuses,
large and small.

ISBN 978-0-545-28867-5

12 11 10 9 8 7 6 5 4 3 2 1   10 11 12 13 14 15/0

Printed in Singapore   46

First Scholastic printing, September 2010

Design by Katrina Damkoehler
Text set in Clichee Bold
The art was done in digital ink and digital oil pastel.